This book belongs to

Young Readers Book Club presents…

A
Week
of Raccoons

by Gloria Whelan
pictures by Lynn Munsinger

Alfred A. Knopf   New York

For Charles Mercer
—G.W.

For Dan
—L.M.

Grolier Enterprises Inc. offers a varied selection of
children's book racks and tote bags. For details on
ordering, please write: Grolier Enterprises Inc.,
Sherman Turnpike, Danbury, CT 06816 Attn:
Premium Department

This is a Borzoi Book published by Alfred A. Knopf, Inc.

Published in the United States by Alfred A. Knopf, Inc., New York,
and simultaneously in Canada by Random House of Canada Limited, Toronto.
Distributed by Random House, Inc., New York.

A B C D   0 1 2 3

Library of Congress Cataloging-in-Publication Data
Whelan, Gloria. A week of raccoons.
Summary: Raids on his corn, garbage can,
and bird feeder lead Mr. Twerkle to trap five raccoons and take them out to the
woods, but they refuse to stay where he puts them.
[1. Raccoons—Fiction] I. Munsinger, Lynn, ill. II. Title.
PZ7.W5718We 1988 [E] 87-16800
ISBN 0-394-88396-9 ISBN 0-394-98396-3 (lib. bdg.)

Mr. and Mrs. Twerkle lived in a cottage next to a blue-green pond.

One Sunday morning Mrs. Twerkle called out to her husband, "Edgar, come quickly! Something has knocked over my petunias!"

Mr. Twerkle looked at the pots and frowned. "A raccoon must have been digging in them for grubs," he said. "I'll trap it and take it to the piny woods."

That night Mr. Twerkle put some bacon smeared with peanut butter and sprinkled with sugar in a cage and propped open the trapdoor.

On Monday morning he found a raccoon in the cage. The raccoon looked very annoyed.

Mr. Twerkle put the cage in the back of his pickup truck. He drove along until he came to a tumble-down log cabin. Then he turned and went up a hill to an old apple tree and down the hill to the bridge that crossed the stream and past the little white schoolhouse and the Busbys' farm and into the piny woods, where he let the raccoon go.

When Mr. Twerkle got back, Mrs. Twerkle was waiting for him. "Edgar," she said, "something has tipped over the hummingbird feeder and licked up all the sugar water."

"It must be another raccoon," said Mr. Twerkle. "Don't worry. I'll catch it." That night he baited the cage with bacon, peanut butter, and sugar and set it near the hummingbird feeder.

On Tuesday morning there was another raccoon in the cage. It was smiling sweetly. Mr. Twerkle put the raccoon in the back of his truck and drove along until he came to the tumble-down log cabin. Then he turned and went up the hill to the old apple tree and down the hill to the bridge that crossed the stream and past the little white schoolhouse and the Busbys' farm and into the piny woods, where he let the raccoon go.

When Mr. Twerkle left, the Monday raccoon, who had been sitting on a tree branch sulking, called to the Tuesday raccoon, "How do you like the piny woods?"

"They're all right," said the Tuesday raccoon pleasantly, "but it was nicer living near the blue-green pond. The sugar water there is so tasty."

"Yes," said the Monday raccoon, "and the grubs are so fat. Do you know how to get back there? I can't remember anything," he grumbled, "except going past the Busbys' farm."

"After that you pass the little white schoolhouse," the Tuesday raccoon said, "but I don't remember the rest of the way."

That evening Mr. Twerkle caught a big fish in the blue-green pond. He left it outside the house in a pail of water while he went inside to tell his wife about it.

But when they came to fetch the pail, there was nothing in it but fish
bones. "Another raccoon!" said Mrs. Twerkle.

"Yep," said Mr. Twerkle. He smeared some bacon with peanut butter,
sprinkled sugar on it, and put it in the cage.

On Wednesday morning he found a raccoon asleep in the cage.

He put it in the back of his truck and drove along until he came to the tumble-down log cabin. Then he turned and went up the hill to the old apple tree and down the hill to the bridge that crossed the stream and past the little white schoolhouse and the Busbys' farm and into the piny woods, where he let the raccoon go.

When Mr. Twerkle was gone, the Monday raccoon and the Tuesday raccoon came out of hiding. "Welcome to the woods!" they said.

"Thanks," said the Wednesday raccoon. "Too bad there aren't any fish here," he added with a big yawn.

"There isn't any sugar water either," said the Tuesday raccoon.

"Nor any grubs," said the Monday raccoon. "We'd like to get back to the blue-green pond, but we don't know where to go after you pass the Busbys' farm and the little white schoolhouse."

"I believe you cross the bridge over the stream," said the Wednesday raccoon drowsily, "but I don't know the rest of the way." And he dropped off to sleep.

After their lunch on Wednesday, Mrs. Twerkle asked Mr. Twerkle
to take the garbage out to the garbage can. Mr. Twerkle found the garbage
can tipped over and the garbage scattered all over the yard.
Mr. Twerkle sighed and baited the cage.

On Thursday morning he found a raccoon in the cage, licking peanut butter off its whiskers. Mr. Twerkle put the cage in the back of his truck and drove along until he came to the tumble-down log cabin. Then he turned and went up the hill to the old apple tree and down the hill to the bridge that crossed the stream and past the little white schoolhouse and the Busbys' farm and into the piny woods, where he let the raccoon go.

As soon as his truck disappeared, three raccoons climbed down from their trees.

"Hi."

"Hi."

"Hi."

"Hi, yourselves," said the Thursday raccoon, carefully smoothing his fur. "It's shady here in the woods, but there isn't any garbage."

"There aren't any fish either," said the Wednesday raccoon.

"Nor any sugar water," said the Tuesday raccoon.

"And not a single grub," said the Monday raccoon. "We want to get back to the blue-green pond, but we don't know where to go after the Busbys' farm and the little white schoolhouse and the bridge over the stream."

"You go up the hill to the old apple tree," said the Thursday raccoon, "but I don't remember the rest of the way."

That afternoon Mr. and Mrs. Twerkle put on their straw hats and went out to the garden to hoe their corn. But when they got there, the cornstalks were lying on the ground and all the tender ears of corn had been eaten. "Another raccoon!" cried the Twerkles. Mrs. Twerkle ran for the bacon.

On Friday morning there was a raccoon in the cage, picking its teeth.

Without a word, Mr. Twerkle put the cage in the back of his truck and drove along until he came to the tumble-down log cabin. Then he turned and went up the hill to the old apple tree and down the hill to the bridge that crossed the stream and past the little white schoolhouse and the Busbys' farm and into the piny woods, where he let the raccoon go.

As soon as Mr. Twerkle drove away, four raccoons popped out of the trees.

"Hi."

"Hi."

"Hi."

"Hi."

"Hi to you," said the Friday raccoon. "Is there any corn in these woods? I'm awfully hungry."

"Probably not," said the Thursday raccoon. "There isn't even any decent garbage." Then he looked hopefully at the Friday raccoon. "I don't suppose you know how to get back to the blue-green pond after you pass the Busbys' farm and the little white schoolhouse and cross the bridge over the stream and go up the hill to the old apple tree, do you?"

"As a matter of fact I do," said the Friday raccoon. "You go to the tumble-down log cabin. From there it's only a short way to the blue-green pond."

"Let's go!" said all five raccoons at once.

They left the piny woods and made their way to the Busbys' farm.
"My," said the Friday raccoon, admiring Mr. Busby's cornfield, "I don't
believe I've ever seen so many rows of corn. They give me quite an
appetite. I think I'll stay right here." And he did.

The four raccoons continued on to the little white schoolhouse. "Look at the huge garbage can on the back porch of the little white schoolhouse," the Thursday raccoon said. "I'll bet it's full of tasty orange peels and apple cores. I'm going to stay right here." And he did.

Next the three raccoons came to the bridge that crossed over the stream.
The Wednesday raccoon had been feeling rather sleepy, so he poked
his nose into the cold water to wake himself up. "Fish!" he cried. "The
biggest ones I've ever seen! I'm going to stay right here." And he did.

As the two raccoons made their way up the hill a bee flew over their heads. "Hmm," said the Tuesday raccoon. "Where there are bees there must be honey." He followed the bee to a hollow in the old apple tree. It was full of wild honey. "This is even sweeter than sugar water," he said with a big smile. "I'm going to stay right here." And he did.

The Monday raccoon loped down the hill all by himself to the tumble-down cabin. Feeling a little grumpy, he kicked over one of the tumble-down logs. "Well, that's more like it!" he cried. "Look at all the nice fat grubs under this log! I believe I'll stay right here." And he did.

On Saturday morning Mr. and Mrs. Twerkle hurried to their window
and peered out.

The petunias were in their pots. The hummingbird feeder was full of sugar water. The fish Mr. Twerkle had caught the night before was swimming in the pail. The lid was still on the garbage can, and a new row of corn had ripened in the garden.

"Well, Edgar, I guess you can put the cage away," said Mrs. Twerkle.

"Yep," said Mr. Twerkle. And he did.